LEVEL 3 READER

W9-CCC-816

Scavenger Hunt

By Gabrielle Reyes
Illustrated by The Artifact Group

SCHOLASTIC INC.

ISBN 978-0-545-59209-3

12 11 10 9 8 7 6 5 4 3 2 1   13 14 15 16 17 18/0

Designed by Angela Jun

Printed in the U.S.A.   40

First printing, September 2013

"Gather around, puppies! We're just about ready," Kirby barked.

The triplets, Kirby, Dozer, and Bernie, had planned a fun day for their friends. "Fall is our favorite season," explained Dozer, "so we're having a scavenger hunt to celebrate!"

Bernie jumped in excitedly. "You have to find the clues we hid all over Puppyville. Each clue will be a riddle. When you figure it out, you'll know where to find the next clue."

"It's going to be so much fun!" Kirby added. "When you get to the end, we have a special surprise!"

"*Ooh!*" Gigi whispered to Peanut. "*J'adore* scavenger hunts! I just love them!"

"Me, too," Peanut agreed. "Plus, I can use my new camera!"

"Now for your first clue," Kirby said. He read from a piece of paper:

"When it starts to get cold, what could be better than looking in here for a cozy fall sweater?"

"*Hmm . . .*" said Spike. "We have to think about where we would find a fall sweater. . . . Hey! I've got an idea. Puppies, follow me!"

"Of course! The closet!" Montana exclaimed. Inside, fuzzy sweaters hung on hangers, bright scarves hung on hooks, and piles of hats sat on a shelf.

"I love it when the weather gets chilly and I can wear fall accessories," Ivy said, wrapping a striped scarf around her neck.

"This cap will be part of my fall look," said Fuji, admiring herself in the mirror.

"Look this way, Fuji!" said Peanut, snapping a photo.

"*Ooh!* This sweater is so soft and warm!" Montana squealed.

She turned so Peanut could take a picture, putting her paw in her pocket to strike a pose. "Whoa, what's this?" she asked pulling out a folded piece of paper. She gasped. "Puppies! I found it—the second clue!"

The puppies crowded around Montana as she read:
"*To find the clue, look under these—*
falling bits of pretty orange trees."
"But . . ." Ivy thought hard. ". . . we don't have any orange trees in Puppyville. Only apple trees."

While Peanut was thinking about the clue, he noticed the funny hat Spike was wearing and took a picture.

"Puppies, I've got it!" Gigi said, clapping her paws. "This way!" she barked and scampered out the door.

Spike and Peanut followed their friends to the backyard where Gigi stood proudly. The leaves had changed color and had been falling off the trees for weeks.

"We don't have orange trees, but we *do* have trees with orange *leaves*!" Gigi exclaimed. "The clue said to look 'under falling bits of pretty orange trees.' Let's look through these piles! I bet the next clue is in here."

Ivy jumped into the nearest pile and leaves went flying. One landed right on Gigi's nose.

"Hey, Ivy! Look what you did!" said Gigi, laughing.

"Ha-ha! Don't move!" Peanut framed his camera and took a closeup. Then he noticed Montana and Fuji having a competition to see who could jump the highest. He snapped another picture, then another. Suddenly, he heard Ivy shout.

"Here it is!"

Ivy shook the leaves off her body and read the clue:
*"It's the greatest place to spend the day.
Let's slide and swing. Let's spin and play!"*

"Let's think. . . ." said Ivy. "Where can we slide, swing, spin, and play?"

"Oh, I know!" yelped Fuji. "I bet it means the Puppyville Park playground!"

I haven't found a clue yet, Peanut thought to himself. *I hope I find the next one.*

When the gang arrived at the park, Peanut and his friends spotted the triplets.

"Over here, pups!" called Bernie.

The group walked toward the open area next to the playground where Bernie, Dozer, and Kirby had set up baskets. Several feet away, they saw little red sacks that looked like apples.

"I love apples in the fall, so we're going to play an apple-toss game," Bernie explained. "The first puppy to get all five 'apples' into the basket will get the last clue of our scavenger hunt."

Each puppy ran to take a spot near a basket. "Toss
me an apple, Peanut!" called Spike. Peanut threw a
red sack to his friend. Spike bumped it off his nose
straight into the air, then kicked up his hind legs, so
the sack bounced off his back.

"That was awesome, Spike!" said Peanut. "I got a
perfect shot of it, too."

"Good one, Spike," Gigi called. "But watch *moi*, Peanut!" Gigi hopped back onto her hind legs and balanced the sack on her nose.

"*Whoa!* Hold that pose!" Peanut directed. *Click!* Just then, they heard the triplets cheering.

"Congratulations, Ivy! You got all the apples in the basket," Bernie said. "Here's the last clue!"

"Oh, no!" Peanut groaned. He had been so busy taking pictures of his friends that he hadn't even gotten one sack in his basket.

Peanut sat down sadly as he listened to Ivy read the last clue:

"*Autumn days are fun and sweet.*
Head to Puppyville Manor for one last treat!"

Back at Puppyville Manor, Ivy, Montana, Fuji, Spike, Gigi, and Peanut gathered in the living room while the triplets prepared their surprise in the kitchen.

Fuji noticed that Peanut was slumped in front of the computer, uploading pictures from his camera.

"What's wrong, Peanut?" Fuji asked.

"I didn't find any of the clues today," Peanut said with a sigh. "I was too busy taking pictures."

Fuji looked at the screen full of the amazing photos Peanut had taken. "Don't be sad, Peanut," said Fuji, brightening. "I have an idea!" She ran into the kitchen before Peanut could say another word.

"We hope you had a great day today," Dozer said a few minutes later. "Kirby, Bernie, and I have prepared a special surprise." He winked at Kirby, who dimmed the lights. Then Fuji hit a key on the computer. A slideshow of Peanut's photos from the day filled the screen.

All the puppies came running over.

"That hat looks *fantastique* on you, Fuji," said Gigi.

"Look how high you jumped!" Spike said to Montana.

"Great trick, Spike!" said Kirby.

"Thanks for capturing all the fun, Peanut," said Fuji. "Now our scavenger hunt is truly unforgettable!"

"We made apple donuts for everyone," Dozer said. "This first one is for you, Peanut."

"But before you take a bite, let *me* take a picture of *you*!" said Fuji with a grin. Say . . . *donut!*"